THE TUSHY BOOK

FRAN MANUSHKIN   ILLUSTRATED BY TRACY DOCKRAY

FEIWEL AND FRIENDS
NEW YORK

L ife is comfy, you will find,
when you have your own behind.

Sitting down would **NOT** be cushy
if you didn't have your tushy!
When you're born, your tushy's there,
ready to go anywhere.

After crawling,

you can nap.

Your tushy fits
on every lap.

Tushies! Tushies! Riding sleds,
somersaulting over heads.
Tushies small or tushies plump,
pillow you on every bump!

Every tushy's in the back.
Every tushy has a crack!
Where would you put underwear
if your tushy wasn't there?

Tushy's so much fun to say.
Say it ten times every day:

TUSHY! TUSHY!

TUSHY! TUSHY

TUSHY!

TUSHY!

When you sleep,
your tushy's lying.

When you leap,
your tushy's flying!

Tushies dancing!

Skating!

Spinning!

Tushies racing!
Tushies **WINNING!**

Every dog and every kitty
needs a tush for sitting pretty!

Kings and queens
have tushies, too.
You can't see them,
but they do!

Grown-up tushies, firm or droopy.
Baby tushies, cute but poopy!
Tushies dressed and tushies bare.
Tushies, tushies **EVERYWHERE**.

So be happy!
Jump and cheer!
You will always have your rear!
Stand up tall!
Be proud to say:

I use my tushy

EVERY DAY!

To Katherine Anne Woo and to Sandra Jordan—with lots of love!
—F. M.

To Parker, who has one of the cutest tushies I know.
—T. D.

A Feiwel and Friends Book
An Imprint of Macmillan

Library of Congress Cataloging-in-Publication Data

Manushkin, Fran.
The tushy book / by Fran Manushkin ; illustrated by Tracy Dockray. — 1st ed.
p. cm.
Summary: Pictures and verse praise the virtues of the bottom.
ISBN-13: 978-0-312-36926-2 / ISBN-10: 0-312-36926-3
[1. Stories in rhyme.   2. Buttocks—Fiction.]   I. Dockray, Tracy, ill.   II. Title.
PZ8.3.M3565Tu 2009   [E]—dc22   2008028544

The art was created with pencil and transparent inks on vellum.
Book design by Tracy Dockray and Barbara Grzeslo
Feiwel and Friends logo designed by Filomena Tuosto

First Edition: April 2009

10 9 8 7 6 5 4 3 2 1

www.feiwelandfriends.com